A Daisy at the Beach

A Daisy at the Beach

By Holly Anna • Illustrated by Genevieve Santos

LITTLE SIMON
New York London Toronto Sydney New Delhi

LITTLE SIMON

An imprint of Simon & Schuster Children's Publishing Division
1230 Avenue of the Americas, New York, New York 10020
First Little Simon paperback edition July 2019
Copyright © 2019 by Simon & Schuster, Inc.
Also available in a Little Simon hardcover edition.
All rights reserved, including the right of reproduction in whole or in part in any form.
LITTLE SIMON is a registered trademark of Simon & Schuster, Inc., and associated colophon is a trademark of Simon & Schuster, Inc. For information about special discounts for bulk purchases, please contact Simon & Schuster Special Sales at 1-866-506-1949 or business@simonandschuster.com. The Simon & Schuster Speakers Bureau can bring authors to your live event. For more information or to book an event contact the Simon & Schuster Speakers Bureau at 1-866-248-3049 or visit our website at www.simonspeakers.com.
Designed by Laura Roode
Manufactured in the United States of America 0220 MTN
2 4 6 8 10 9 7 5 3
Library of Congress Cataloging-in-Publication Data
Names: Anna, Holly, author. | Santos, Genevieve, illustrator.
Title: A Daisy at the beach / by Holly Anna ; illustrated by Genevieve Santos.
Description: First Little Simon paperback edition. | New York : Little Simon, 2019. | Series: Daisy dreamer ; #10 | Summary: While spending the day at the beach, Daisy's imaginary friend Posey turns her into a mermaid and they help a lost octopus reunite with her friends.
Identifiers: LCCN 2019011405 | ISBN 9781534442610 (paperback) | ISBN 9781534442627 (hardcover) | ISBN 9781534442634 (eBook)
Subjects: | CYAC: Beaches—Fiction. | Imaginary playmates—Fiction. | Mermaids—Fiction. | Octopuses—Fiction. | Lost and found possessions—Fiction. | Imagination—Fiction. | Magic—Fiction. | BISAC: JUVENILE FICTION / Imagination & Play. | JUVENILE FICTION / Humorous Stories. | JUVENILE FICTION / Readers / Chapter Books.
Classification: LCC PZ7.1.A568 Daf 2019 | DDC [Fic]—dc23
LC record available at https://lccn.loc.gov/2019011405

CONTENTS

CHAPTER ONE

Road Trip!

"Wow, Daisy Dreamer! You look beachy cool!" I say to the me in the mirror. I am wearing my favorite bathing suit. It has colorful stripes and *spaghetti* straps. But not *real* spaghetti. *Obviously.*

Why am I dressed in a bathing suit? Because today I'm going to the *beach*! And when you go to the beach, you have to go to the beach in style.

I sway my hips and pretend to be a hula girl, moving my arms from left to right. I can almost hear the music playing, but my cat, Sir Pounce, looks at me like I'm a weirdo.

Enough hula dancing for now! Time to pack my beach bag. I have a super-long list of things to take to the beach:

TO PACK

- ☐ Mermaid Beach Towel
- ☐ Sparkly Strawberry-Scented Sunscreen
- ☐ Heart-Shaped movie-star sunglasses
- ☐ Over-the-rainbow striped folding beach chair
- ☐ Boogie-woogie boogie board

Hmmm. I tap my head thoughtfully. Did I forget anything? Then I snap my fingers and write down: Book.

☑ Boogie-woogie boogie board
☑ Starfish sand buckets
☑ Neon green and yellow shovels
☑ Swim goggles
☐ Book ♡

And oh yeah! One more thing! I race out of my bedroom and lean over the railing. "MOM!" I shout at the top of my lungs. "Do you have my beach umbrella?" I wait for an answer.

"All packed, honey!" Mom shouts back.

I scramble to my room and . . . *Oh no!* Sir Pounce has packed himself in my beach bag. My secret spy cat has detected I'm going somewhere. I grab him around the middle and pull him right out of my bag.

"You can't go to the beach, silly!" I say, shaking my finger at him. "You might get *lost*."

"Mrr-row," Sir Pounce meows.

He doesn't like packing, because suitcases and bags mean I'm going away. Sir Pounce doesn't like it when I go *anywhere*. *Obviously*. One time my wild kitty tried to unpack my camp trunk and got my underwear stuck on his head. He looked like a masked superhero. Hilarious!

"Hey!" I cry as Sir Pounce swipes my goggles and runs away. I chase him around my room. He hops onto my bed and . . . and *whoa*! Sir Pounce suddenly freezes in midair! He is floating above my bed.

I put my hands on my hips and scan my room. This floating cat trick has imaginary friend magic written *all* over it.

"Posey? Come out, come out, wherever you are!" I call.

Then I spy an antler sticking out
from under the dust ruffle.

I tap it and say, "There you are!"

Posey wiggles out from under my
bed. He is my imaginary friend from

the World of Make-Believe, and when he's around, crazy things happen. Like cats floating in the air.

He gives me a wave. "Hi, Daisy! Whatcha doing?"

Before I can answer, there's a loud "MEOW." Posey and I look up at Sir Pounce.

"I think he wants down," I say.

Posey snaps his fingers, and Sir Pounce drifts down to the bed and begins to purr. *Silly kitty!*

Then I tell Posey that I'm packing for the beach, and I also tell him how much Sir Pounce dislikes packing. And you know what Posey does? He starts playfully meowing at my cat. They meow, hiss, and cough back and forth to each other.

Finally Posey turns to me and asks, "Can we go to the beach with you?"

I arch an eyebrow. "What do you mean, 'we'?"

Sir Pounce and Posey share a look.

"Oh, did I say 'we'?" Posey says nervously. "I meant 'me.' Can *me* go to the beach with you?"

And even though he is totally using bad English, I can't resist Posey's awesome idea to join me at the beach. We'll have twice the fun! *Obviously.*

CHAPTER TWO

Seas the Day!

First I make Posey promise me one
thing.

"You *have* to stay invisible at the
beach," I say, staring him right in the
eye. "Because not everyone is used to
seeing an imaginary friend."

Posey snaps his fingers and
becomes invisible. Now only *I* can see
him. *Obviously.*

We finish packing up everything
and drag my load of stuff—*ka-bonk,
ka-bonk, ka-bonk*—downstairs.

I help Dad pack the car, and Posey behaves like the perfect imaginary friend. He doesn't get me in trouble once. *Phew!* Then we buckle up and wave to Sir Pounce, who's sitting in the living room window. He's pawing the glass.

As we whiz down the highway, Posey loves looking out the window. He bounces up and down when we pass the curvy slides at the water park. He presses his nose against the window when we go by Santa Land. He even waves to the floppy, air-dancing tube guy in front of the car dealership.

My dad hangs a left at the giant seahorse, and now I *know* we're *super* close to the beach. I crack the window and breathe in the air. It smells like the sea!

Soon we pull into the parking lot. I hop out of the car and slip on my flip-flops. Then I grab my bag and let Mom and Dad walk ahead of us.

"Ready?" I ask Posey. He nods and steps onto the sand.

"YEOWCH!" he yells.

"Keep it down, dude!" I say.

But Posey takes off, doing a hot lava dance all the way to the water.

"Ahhhhhhhh," Posey moans as he cools his hot feet in the sea. "Why is the beach made of hot, squeaky dirt?"

I laugh and pick up a fistful of sand. "This is not dirt," I tell him. "It's sand. And you're going to love it."

"I doubt that," Posey complains as he steps carefully out of the ocean.

"Suit yourself," I say, picking a spot near the water to spread out my towel and set up my chair. My parents can see me, but Posey and I can also still be private.

I plunk onto my chair, slip on my heart-shaped movie-star glasses, and put on my sparkly strawberry-scented sunscreen. Posey lies down on his own invisible towel beside me.

"What do you think of the beach?" I ask.

Posey rolls over and props himself up on one elbow. "Well, I like the sound of the waves, and the wind feels nice—but what do people do here? I'm bored."

So much for relaxing, I think. But that's okay. I can't wait to show Posey how much fun it is at the beach.

"We can do whatever you want to do," I say.

Posey pulls a shovel out of my bag and smiles. "I want to build a sandcastle!"

☆ Chapter Three ☆

Dream Castles

"Not to brag," I tell him, "but I am a *master* at sandcastles."

Posey hops to his feet. "Tell me your secrets of the sand!" he cries.

I move back a little from the water.

"First you have to find the right spot to build your castle," I explain. "It can't be too close to the water or the tide will wash it away."

Posey nods.

"You also need water to make your castle," I continue. "So I always dig a hole down to the water, like this."

I take my shovel and begin to dig a hole. Posey watches closely. I scoop and scoop the sand. The deeper I dig,

the wetter the sand gets. Soon I hit
water.

Posey peeks into the hole. "Wow!
Now what?"

"Now we need an umbrella," I say.
I pull out my umbrella and twist it
into the ground.

"Umbrella?" Posey asks. "Are you expecting *rain*?"

I laugh. "No, silly! This is a *sun* umbrella. It makes it shady so we won't get too hot while we're making our castles."

Posey gives me two purple thumbs-up.

"The first thing you make is the castle's moat," I tell him, digging a big circle in the sand. "Then you build your castle on the area *inside* the moat."

I reach into my water well and pull out fistfuls of wet sand and fill my bucket. I mix in some dry sand so it's not too soupy. Then I pack the sand firmly and turn over my bucket.

"Ta-da!" I cry. "One castle tower."

Posey frowns at my tower. "How are you going to build a whole giant castle with one bucket of sand at a time? It'll take *forever*. And how will it fit in your tiny circle?"

"Wait," I say to Posey. "We are not building a *life-size* castle, silly. Sandcastles are *miniature* castles."

Posey taps the side of his head with his finger. "*Ooooh, now I get it!*"

Then we both get to work. I make two more towers, an archway, and some drippy spires. Then I fill my moat with water and decorate my castle with seashells. That's when I notice Posey's castle.

Oh. My. Gosh. His sandcastle is *huge*. It has watchtowers, arches, balconies, a working drawbridge, and actual windows. It even has a very tiny, but *very real*, king and queen! And a knight blowing a trumpet!

"Meet the royal family of Oceana!" Posey says proudly.

My mouth drops open like a drawbridge.

"Did I do it right?" Posey asks.

I gulp loudly. "To be honest," I say, "most sandcastles do not have *tiny* people living inside them."

"Oh . . . sorry!" Posey apologizes as he flings magic dust on his castle, and— *poof!*—the king, queen, and knight turn to sand, but now I hear a soft "meow" come from inside his castle.

Dear Posey. What have you done now?

☆ ✩ CHAPTER FOUR ☆

Beach Kitty

Posey holds his hands out in front of me like a stop sign.

"Before you freak out, I think you should know something," he says. "I can speak cat."

I roll my eyes. "What does that have to do with building sandcastles?"

Then the drawbridge creaks open, and Sir Pounce's cat face peeks out.

"Explain," I say firmly.

Posey talks fast. "It's just that Sir Pounce really wanted to go to the beach. He doesn't like to miss out on all the fun! And when he was pawing the window, he wasn't saying good-bye, he was asking you to bring him along."

Sir Pounce looks at me. "Mrr-row!"

I soften ever so slightly.

Wow, I think. I had no idea Sir Pounce actually wanted to go with me on trips. That's pretty cool. But wait! "Pets are not allowed at the beach!"

Posey smiles slyly and asks, "What about invisible pets?"

With a snap of his fingers, Sir Pounce disappears. Completely.

"Mrr-row!" says the nothing space where my cat used to be.

I roll my eyes *again*. "Can you at least make him visible to just *us*?"

Posey tosses some imaginary friend dust at the castle door. And wa-la! Sir Pounce reappears on the drawbridge. I can almost see him smile.

Then he hops over the moat and starts talking to Posey in cat.

And I'm not going to lie—I feel super *left out*. I tap my foot on the sand. "What are you two talking about?"

Posey turns to me. "We're talking about the rules."

I keep tapping my foot. "What rules?"

Posey puts his arm around Sir Pounce. "Your cat has promised not to run away, and he will also obey all your orders."

I sigh heavily. I just want a nice day at the beach. Then I realize that maybe having Sir Pounce here would be awesome. Just the thought of it gives me a little surge of excitement. Then I fling two fistfuls of sand in the air.

"Okay," I say, giving in. "Let the beach party begin!"

☆ Chapter Five ☆

Mermaid Dreams

Sir Pounce thinks the beach is a giant kitty litter box.

"No! No! No!" I keep reminding him, because I do not want to play next to a pile of . . . um, gross stuff in the sand.

Finally Posey meow-explains everything in cat, and Sir Pounce nods.

"He's good," Posey tells me.

"It's your first time at the beach," I say. "What do *you* want to do?"

Posey meows the translation. *Obviously.* Sir Pounce meows back.

"He would like to dip his paws in the water," Posey informs me.

This may sound like an odd request, because most cats hate water. But not my cat. He *loves* water.

"Race you to the waves!" I yell, taking off for the surf.

Sir Pounce and Posey chase after me. I splash over the little waves and flop—stomach first—into the water. Sir Pounce jumps in beside me, and Posey stands by the water's edge.

"Come in!" I cry. "The water feels great!"

But Posey doesn't want to get wet. He says he doesn't like to feel soggy and damp.

"Use your *magic!*" I suggest.

A smile spreads across his purple face, and he grabs a fistful of sparkly imaginary friend dust and flings it over his head.

"Whoop-de-do!" he shouts.

Then—*poof!*—Posey is magically wearing a scuba mask and fins. He charges into the water, and when he comes up for air, his fur is perfect.

Now that's some pretty fabulous magic! I think.

We wander into the waves—but not too far. We can still touch the bottom. A swell comes, and we ride it all the way back to the beach.

"Again!" I cry.

Then we race out into the surf and ride another wave to shore. We're on our way again when Posey points to something farther out.

"Did you see *that*?" he exclaims.

Sir Pounce and I look in the direction Posey's pointing.

WHAP! A fish jumps in front of us and slaps back into the water.

"People live in the ocean!" Posey says with a gasp.

I giggle. "Not people, but there are animals that do."

Can you imagine what it would be like if we lived in the ocean? Personally, I know I would love it. I decide to share a secret.

"I know this may sound silly," I say. "But I've always wanted to be a mermaid."

I wait for Posey and Sir Pounce to laugh at me, but they don't laugh at all! Instead, a sneaky grin sweeps across Posey's face. He gets this look when he's about to say something wild. *Okay, get ready for it, Daisy. Here it comes . . . !*

Posey raises his eyebrows and asks, "How would you like to be a *mermaid* for a day?"

Chapter Six

Mer-mazing!

I don't have to think about it at all. I just grab my head with both hands and shout, "Y-E-S spells 'yes,'" and *sha-zing*! Posey makes my wish come true!

There's a blue-green fish tail where my legs used to be. It's very soft and smooth to the touch. I gently wave the tail up and down, which makes me glide through the water.

I can't explain it, but I feel like I have been a mermaid my whole life!

Swoooooshh! I dive underwater to admire my shimmering tail. It winks in the sunlight. I have become a graceful, bedazzled sea angel.

Swish! Swoosh! I dart this way and that. I look behind me and spy a cute orange fish chasing my tail.

"MRR-ROW!" says the fish as it catches up.

Wait, I think. Can fish speak cat too?

But when the orange fish nuzzles against me, I know that we've met before.

"Sir Pounce!" I cheer. "Posey turned you into a fish!"

"MRR-row!" the fish repeats happily.

Posey flippers to my side and says, "You look mer-mazing!"

I *feel* mer-mazing too. Not only because I am a mermaid, but because I am breathing and talking underwater!

"What do we do now?" I ask.

Posey motions to the deep, dark water around us. "Let's watch the show."

In the distance, a group of jellyfish swims our way with pulsing bodies. Some have twinkly lights inside their umbrella-shaped bells. I watch their colorful stingers trailing behind them like party streamers. I steer clear of those stingers to be on the safe side.

Next, a sea turtle swims up beside me with a curious look. We paddle side by side. Colorful fish dart all around us. Each fish is like a little work of art, with rings, spots, or stripes. Underneath us, pink, orange, and purple sea stars cling to a coral reef. A manta ray wafts along with the current.

"This is so magical!" I cry.

Posey nods as he sits on a rock watching all the fish. Then something silly happens. The rock Posey's sitting on opens up! It's a giant sea clam! Posey falls off, and I laugh so hard a stream of bubbles trails from my mouth.

As I help Posey up, Sir Pounce darts from my side, chasing after a fish. With a swish of my tail, I catch up to Sir Pounce and shake my head.

"You have to be *kind* to the sea creatures," I tell him. "Remember, we are visiting *their* world."

So Sir Pounce turns around and chases *me* instead. *Zip! Zoop! Za-room!* We play hide-and-seek on the reef. Posey joins us.

We are having so much fun! But then I see something huge and dark in the shadows, and I know it's time for a new adventure.

☆ Chapter Seven ☆

Shipwreck Garden

I swim a little closer to see what's lurking in the shadows. Posey and Sir Pounce follow me.

"It's a shipwreck!" I cry.

The old ship rests on its side. I count three masts. Long seaweed fronds have grown on the hull. They waft gently in the current. A school of small fish swims from the cabin.

I see a crab scuttle into a hole in the wood while spiky sea urchins cling to the sides of the ship.

"Wow, this boat has become a home for sea creatures!" I say.

"And look!" yelps Posey. "There are *brains* growing on the deck!"

"Those are not *real* brains," I say. *Obviously.* "It's brain coral. And I also see purple sea anemones."

Posey crosses his eyes. "Purple *what*?"

I giggle because it *is* such a hard name.

"*Ah-nem-oh-nee!*" I repeat slowly. "It looks like a pretty flower, but *don't* touch it! It stings like a jellyfish."

Posey swims away from the wiggly anemones to check out a rusty old anchor lying on the sand.

"Does this animal sting?" he asks.

"No, that's an anchor, not an animal," I explain. "It holds the ship down in place."

Posey nods and tells the anchor, "Well, you are doing a very good job."

Quietly, a strange new creature slips out from the ship. It's an eight-armed cutie-pie octopus!

"Hi, there!" I say, but the octopus swishes away in a cloud of ink. *Oh no! I must have frightened it.*

But Posey says something that

I can barely hear, and the octopus stops. It points its tentacles at itself. Posey speaks again, and the octopus inches back.

Well, I'll be a deep-sea diver. Posey knows how to speak octopus, too. *Obviously.*

"Daisy, this is Inky," Posey says, introducing the octopus. "She is lost and can't find her friends."

Inky waves to me with all her arms, and I wave back with one hand. "I'm sorry to hear you are lost. Can we help?"

The octopus lets out a murmur that is too low for my mermaid ears. Then Posey snaps his fingers and sprinkles imaginary friend dust over us.

This time I hear Inky's voice loud and clear. "Yes, please!"

Chapter Eight

Sea Ghost

I, Daisy Dreamer, am now a mermaid in detective mode.

"Inky, have you tried retracing your steps?" I ask.

"No," Inky says nervously.

"That's okay," I say. "What have you seen since you lost your friends?"

Inky looks at us with her big round octopus eyes as she thinks.

"Well, I remember a garden of orange and purple sea stars. Before that, I heard the sounds of a murky song. I also saw a treasure chest sticking up from the sand." Inky looks down at the ocean floor sadly. "And that was the last time I saw my friends."

I flick my fish tail.

"Those are great clues!" I say.
"Let's see if we can find them and get
you back home."

To start our search, Posey asks a school of sardines if they've seen any of the clues. But they flicker by without stopping.

"Those fish are too busy to answer me," Posey says.

"That's because they're in school all day," I say. "Get it?"

Posey shakes his head and rolls his eyes.

Suddenly Sir Pounce darts away again, probably chasing more fish. Doesn't he know we are on a mission?

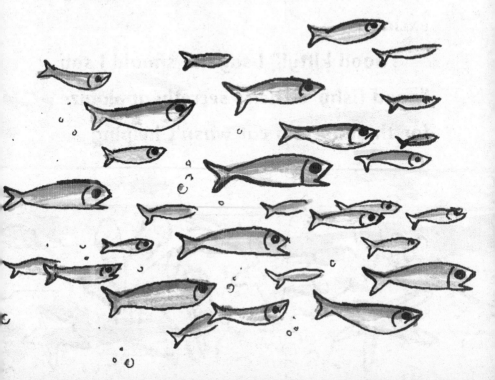

But Posey takes my hand and one of Inky's tentacles. "He wants to show us something!"

We swim after Sir Pounce, who leads us right to a garden of orange and purple sea stars.

"You found the first clue!" Inky exclaims.

"Good kitty!" I say. Or should I say "good fishy"? Then I secretly apologize for thinking my cat wasn't helping.

Inky holds a tentacle up. "The murky song was near the sea stars. Can you hear anything?"

We stop and listen quietly. Then a strange melody washes in.

"*Woo-OOO-ooo!*"

Something in the distance wails and echoes all around us. I look at my friends, and our eyes all grow wide. We stay quiet.

"Woo-OOO-ooo!"

Now everyone hides behind me.

"It sounds like an underwater ghost," Posey whispers. "And it will probably sting us!"

The song takes me back to a video I saw once about the largest animals in the sea. My eyes almost pop out of my head with excitement because now I know just what this sound is!

"That's no ghost," I say. "It's a whale!"

☆ Chapter Nine ☆

Hidden Treasure

Posey looks embarrassed. "I guess I need to brush up on my whale sounds."

We swim toward the singing until a giant humpback whale emerges from the ocean shadows.

"Well, here's your chance!" I say.

Inky wraps each of her eight arms around me.

"I'm scared," she whispers.

I hug her back and say, "I can tell. Don't worry, Inky. If anyone can handle this, it's Posey."

And I'm right! Posey sings, grunts, and whistles with the whale. Is there nothing my imaginary friend can't do?

After they talk for what feels like forever, the whale finally swims slowly on, and Posey floats back to our side.

"Well, that was Humpfrey," he tells us. "What a really nice whale he was! He had a lot to say. We talked about how much fun splashing is. And he gets to spit out water from his head. How cool is that? Oh, and then he said something about a treasure chest."

"A treasure chest!" both Inky and I echo.

Posey smiles. "Yeah, it's buried right underneath us."

I look down, but all I can see is sand, seaweed, and muck. We swim to the bottom and wipe our hands over the soft ground until we find something hard. It's the corner of a chest!

Posey, Inky, and Sir Pounce help me scoop up the sand. The deeper we dig, the stinkier and gloppier the muck gets. Posey and I free the treasure chest from the mud and drag it to where the water is clear.

"Is this the same treasure chest you saw, Inky?" I ask.

Inky shrugs. "Maybe. Should we open it?"

Um, the answer to this question is always yes. *Obviously.*

We pull it open. Inside the chest are stunning, sea-polished shells! Orange lion's paws. Pearly abalone shells. Yellow limpets. Shimmering sand dollars. Purple sea scallops. They are beautiful.

As we dig through the treasure, Inky's octopus friends swim up! Inky links tentacles with her friends, and they dance around in a circle.

"We've been looking for you everywhere!" one of her friends says.

Inky laughs. "And I was looking for you!"

Posey and I watch Inky and her friends. She is so happy to be home. It makes me miss my home too. That's when I hear my name drifting down to the bottom of the ocean.

"Daisy," my mom's voice rings out.
"Wake up."

A burst of bubbles floods around me, and then I feel a great *whoosh*!

☆ ☆ CHAPTER TEN ☆

Am I Dreaming?

I open my eyes and grab the armrests of my beach chair. *Whoa!* I'm back at the beach! My legs are wrapped in my mermaid beach towel, and I'm sitting under my beach umbrella. I look all around. Posey is gone. Sir Pounce is gone too.

In front of me is a sandcastle that looks *just* like my very own house!

There's a note written in the sand next to it that says *What a FUN day! See you soon!*

Then I watch a wave gently roll over the sand house and note. It washes them both away, and I sigh happily.

Suddenly my mom peers over the umbrella. "Daisy, oh good, you're awake."

I shake my head because I wasn't asleep. Or was I?

Mom smiles at me. "You fell sound asleep in the warm sun. I put your towel over your legs and moved your beach umbrella."

Hmm, was this all just a dream? I wonder. Then I yank off my towel to see if I'm still a mermaid.

Nope. I'm just regular old me.

"Upsy-Daisy!" Mom says. "It's time to go home."

"One more splash!" I say, and I flop into the shallow water. Then I wrap myself back in the towel and race my parents to the parking lot.

I even let them win.

The first thing I do when we get home is check on Sir Pounce. And you know what? That cat is curled up and snoring on my bed!

"Sir Pounce!" I cry, bouncing next to him. "You're not a fish anymore!"

I run my hand over his ears and down his back. Then he stretches, hops onto the floor, and hides under my dust ruffle.

Getting down on my hands and knees, I peek under my bed. "Here, kitty, kitty, kitty!"

Sir Pounce darts out from under my bed and drops something on the floor in front of me. It's a seashell from Inky's treasure chest!

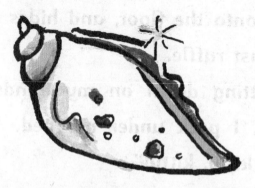

I turn the shell over in my hand. It's *real*!

Sir Pounce curls into my lap and paws at the shell. I give him a kiss on the head and say, "Let's keep this *our* little *sea*-cret."

"Mrr-row!" he meows, and this time I think I understand him.

Check out Daisy Dreamer's next adventure!

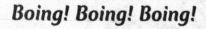

Boing! Boing! Boing!

I, Daisy Dreamer, am hopping around like a bouncy kangaroo. That is how I pull my leggings on for school. *Obviously.* I also like to stretch my waistband out like a kangaroo pouch. Then I let it go. *Thwack!*

Excerpt from *The Bad Luck Day*

As I hippity-hop, I spy a purple blob behind my nightstand. I reach down and grab it!

It's my super-sticky octopus wall walker! It's been missing *for ages*. I got it at a birthday party a long time ago. I squish it in my fist and it smooshes out the sides. Then I hurl it against the wall and watch it crawl to the floor. It looks totally alive!

I run over and grab it and throw it again. And again! Then something crazy, but not totally crazy for me, happens. A door in my wall opens up, and my imaginary friend, Posey, pops out.

"Hi, Daisy!" he cheers.

Posey surprises me right in the middle of winding up to throw, and the wall walker slips out of my hand.

Ka-blammo! The squishy, sticky octopus flies into my desk calendar and knocks it onto the floor. "Oh no, Daisy!" I shout. I always say "Oh no, Daisy" when I knock things over.

Posey laughs and runs over to grab my wall walker. I run after him and pick my calendar up off the floor.

Then I notice the date. "Uh-oh! Today is FRIDAY THE THIRTEENTH!"

Excerpt from *The Bad Luck Day*